Ghost Train

John Goodwin

Stanley Thornes (Publishers) Ltd

D1419039

First published in 1994 by:
Stanley Thornes (Publishers) Ltd
Ellenborough House
Wellington Street
CHELTENHAM GL50 1YW
England

97 98 99 00 / 10 9 8 7 6 5 4

A catalogue record for this book is available from the British Library.

ISBN 0 7487 1877 X

Typeset by Tech-Set, Gateshead
Printed and bound in Great Britain at Martin's The Printers, Berwick

1

I can see the house now. It was big and very old. There was a notice outside saying, 'Danger. Keep out'.

Keep out - that's what we should have done. But we were eight years old, Tim, James and me. We wanted to be big and brave.

We got in through a broken window. The house was cold and damp. There were holes in the floor boards. The walls had big cracks in them. The notice was right. There was danger in this house.

Tim said, 'Let's play hide and seek.'

I really felt afraid of the house. But I didn't say so. I was even more afraid that Tim and James would laugh at me. Instead I said, 'Good idea', and went to hide.

James ran upstairs. I found a large oak door in the hall. I opened it to hide behind it. Suddenly I tripped, and fell down some stairs. I lay on the floor. I couldn't move. My leg was broken.

Then the door slammed shut. There was no light at all - just the evil darkness. Cobwebs brushed my face, and I could feel rats running over me.

I cried out in terror. Nobody came. Nobody heard me.

Tim and James thought I had gone home. I lay for two hours in that hell hole. I could see nothing. I could hear nothing but the rats. I was going mad with fear.

At last someone heard my cries and found me. I was safe. The horror was over. But I never forgot it.

From that day on I have been in terror of being shut in dark places. In my nightmares I still feel the cobwebs. I still feel the rats running over me.

2

It was my birthday. I was twenty-five.

I stood at the fair looking at my girl friend, Jane. She was trying to win a prize on the darts stall. She looked lovely. The bright lights made her long brown hair shine. Her big, dark eyes were full of fun. She was the best birthday present ever.

We were in love and were going to be married. I had never felt so happy in my life before.

Jane wore a large ruby ring on her right hand. It flashed red as she threw a dart. The ring had been left to her by her grandmother. Jane was very proud of it. She said she would never part with it.

I was going to buy her a ring the next day - for her left hand. It would not be worth as much money as the ruby, but Jane said she would be even more proud to wear it.

We went on lots of rides and had a great time. Then everything went wrong. Jane wanted to go on the ghost train.

As soon as she said it, my mind was back in that black cellar. I just couldn't do it. As much as I loved Jane I couldn't go on that ghost train. What made it worse was my pride. I was too proud to tell her about my fear. I was over six feet tall. I was very fit and played football every week. How could I tell Jane I was afraid of the dark? I thought she would laugh at me.

I said, 'I'm hungry. Let's go for something to eat instead.'

Jane said, 'Oh come on, it won't take long! My friend said it's the best ghost train she's ever been on.'

Could I do it? Could I go into the darkness? No, I couldn't. The thought of it made me feel sick with fear. My fear turned into anger. I said, 'Shut up about the ghost train. If you're so keen, go by yourself.'

Jane was upset. 'Is that what you want? Do you really want me to go alone?'

By this time I was really mad at her. 'I don't care who you go with,' I shouted. 'Go with anyone you like!' I turned round and walked away.

That was the biggest mistake of my life. But you are always wise later, aren't you?

3

I walked round the fair for a while. Then I got bored.
My temper had cooled down. I wanted Jane back with
me.

I went to the ghost train to look for her. A lot of people
were waiting to go on the train. Was that Jane by the
pay-box? I could only see her back, but it looked like her.
Then she got on the train with a man. Could she have
found someone else to go with? Was she that mad at me?

I got angry again. This wasn't like Jane. She'd never
gone off with another man before. Even if she was mad at
me, there was no need to go off with someone else! I
could feel my temper rising. Just wait till they got back!

I thought the train would never come back. But at last it
did. I rushed over to it. Lots of people got off. Some
looked afraid. Their faces were white. What had they
seen in that tunnel?

I looked everywhere for Jane. I could see the man who
had been with her. He was tall and he had a deep scar

on his face. But Jane wasn't with him. Where could she be? Was it Jane I had seen, or was it someone else?

I grabbed the man by the arm. 'Where is she?' I asked.

He gave me an odd look. 'Who? What are you talking about?'

I yelled, 'Jane, my girl friend. She got on the ghost train with you. I'm sure she did.'

He laughed. It was an odd sort of laugh and his eyes were cold. 'I was on my own,' he said. 'You've got it all wrong mate. No one was on the train with me!'

I looked around, but there was still no Jane. I didn't know what to think. I said, 'Sorry,' to the man. I didn't feel sorry, but I didn't want him to start a fight. He looked the kind who would.

I began to walk around the fair. I was longing to find Jane. I wanted to hold her close and tell her how much I loved her. I wanted to see her smile and tell me everything was OK. I looked everywhere. I spent hours walking round the fair. I even went on some rides so I could look down on the crowd. But there was no sign of her. By now it was very late and I was tired. If Jane wasn't at the fair, she must be back at her flat. I could call in on my way home.

That's what I did. But Jane wasn't there. I waited outside until 2 a.m. Then I went home to bed. That night I didn't sleep much. When I did, I had lots of bad dreams. Every time I woke up, my first thought was Jane. Where was she? I felt sure she would phone me next morning. But she didn't.

Later on I went round to her flat. I rang the bell. Her landlady came to the door. She knew me. She smiled and asked me in. I asked if Jane was there and she gave me an odd look.

'Didn't you know?' she said slowly. 'Jane has left. She came to get all her things this morning. I was sorry to see her go. She's moving to another town. I don't think she'll come back.'

I asked, 'Was she alone?'

Jane's landlady said, 'No, there was a man with her. He was very tall. He had dark hair and a scar on his face.'

I knew who it was at once. It was the man on the ghost train. He told me that Jane wasn't with him. Why did he lie? Yesterday Jane loved me, but today she had gone off with another man. It just wasn't like her. It didn't add up. Something was wrong. What was happening? Where was Jane? Why did she leave so suddenly? What could I do to get her back?

I'd go to the fair again. Maybe there would be a clue somewhere. I could ask around and talk to people. Someone might know where she was.

I drove to the fairground, but I was too late. The fair had gone. There was nothing left but bits of litter blowing in the wind. No music, no tents, no people - just the cold wind blowing across the field. Something was moving in the grass near to me. It was a poster, blown by the wind. It was an advert for the next town the fair was going to visit. The fair was going to Mayford - and so was I!

4

It was lucky I had some holiday due to me. I asked my boss for the week off. I didn't say what it was for, just that I needed a break. I needed that all right! I got into my car and set off for Mayford.

When I got there, I went in search of the fair. I found it in a field on the outside of town. There were all the noises and smells you always get with a fair. There were hot dogs frying and beefburgers thick with onions. I hadn't eaten all day. Suddenly I felt hungry. I bought a beefburger and went looking for the ghost train.

The woman was at the pay-box. In a way she was good-looking, but she had hard eyes. Would she be able to help me? She must have seen hundreds of people get on and off the ghost train yesterday. Would she remember Jane and the man with the scar?

I was going towards her when I stopped. I could see the man Jane went off with - the man with the scar. He was here at the ghost train. My heart began to beat faster. I wanted to rush up to him and grab him, but that would be stupid. I had to watch and wait.

Scarface went to the woman in the pay-box and spoke to her. She smiled and called out to a giant of a man who was helping people onto the train. 'Here Bill, we can have a break now. Jack says he'll look after the ride for ten minutes.'

So now I knew something about Scarface. His name was Jack and he worked at the fair. Was Jane here as well? If she was, I would soon find her. Scarface went into the pay-box, and Bill and the woman left. I followed them through the crowd until they got to the back of the fair. They went into an old, tatty caravan.

Suddenly there was a lot of shouting. A woman was screaming. My heart missed a beat. It was Jane's voice. I was sure of it!

I ran up to the caravan and banged on the door. The giant opened it and said, 'What do you want?'

I shouted, 'My girl friend is in there with you. I can hear her. Let me see her!'

He said, 'Don't be stupid. It's only me and the wife having a row.'

I yelled, 'It's a lie. I heard Jane's voice. Let me in!'

'Get lost,' he said. 'Get lost, before I call the police!' He slammed the door in my face and I walked back down the steps.

Then I went and hid behind one of the other caravans and watched their door. After ten minutes or so, the man and woman came out of the caravan. The giant looked around him and then locked up.

When they'd gone, I began to walk slowly towards the caravan. I called out softly, 'Jane, are you there? It's me, Paul.' There was no reply. I tapped on the wall of the caravan and called again. If Jane was in there, why didn't she reply?

I walked round the caravan wondering what to do next. Suddenly I saw something shining on the ground. I bent down to pick it up. It was an ear-ring. Did it belong to Jane? There was nothing special about it, but it could be hers. She had a pair just like this.

I had to see if Jane was in that caravan. Somehow I had to look inside. I ran round the caravan and got to the bottom of the steps by the door. Suddenly something hit me hard on the back of the head. The world went spinning round and I passed out!

5

I was back in that dark cellar. This time it was full of ghosts - white ones, flying round the room. A voice said, 'I think he's coming round.' Then I woke up.

I was in hospital. A doctor in a white coat was looking down at me. 'That's a big bump on your head,' he said. 'You must have had quite a fall!'

I said, 'I didn't fall, somebody hit me!'

The doctor smiled. 'Nobody hit you. Sometimes our minds play tricks on us when we pass out. The woman who called the ambulance saw you fall.'

I rubbed my head. Maybe I had slipped over. Maybe it was all in my mind. I didn't know what to think any more.

The doctor said, 'We need to X-ray your head. Then you must stay here for the night, just to be on the safe side.'

'But I must find Jane,' I said. 'I must make sure she's OK.'

The doctor shook his head. 'And I must make sure you're OK. Sorry, but you must stay here tonight.'

6

I woke up the next morning feeling much better. When the doctor saw me, he said I could go home.

The nurse gave me my clothes. They had taken the things out of my pockets, in case they got lost. The nurse handed me a plastic bag. It was all there: my wallet, some loose money and the ear-ring. Jane's ear-ring.

What should I do now? Maybe I should go to the police. But what would I tell them? My girl friend went off with another man. I found her ear-ring. I think someone hit me on the head, but the doctor says I'm all mixed up.

It was a silly story. Even to me it seemed silly. I might as well tell the police that my cat had killed a bird and ask them to arrest it. They would tell me to stop wasting their time.

I had to find Jane myself. No one was going to help me. I didn't want to be seen at the fair, so I waited for it to get dark.

When I got there, the fair was very busy. I went to the boot of my car, and took out a steel bar and a torch. I hid them under my coat. Then I made my way to the ghost train.

I was pleased to see three people minding it: Bill, his wife and Scarface. Scarface looked ugly in the light of the fair - a really mean sort. I didn't like the idea of being caught by him, or Bill.

Still, they couldn't be in two places at once. They were busy, so I could have a good look at their caravan. I hoped Jane was in there more than I've hoped for anything else in my life.

I went to the back of the fair and found the caravan. It was dark now, but no lights were showing. I looked around me. Good, no one was about. I went up the steps and got out the iron bar.

It was a bit of a job breaking in. There was a lot of noise, and it didn't do the door any good. But at last I was inside!

It was really spooky in the caravan. It smelt musty and a bit damp. I turned on the torch and looked around.

Most fairground people are very proud of their homes. They keep everything neat and tidy. But this one was a mess. Everything in the caravan was broken. There were bits of glass all over the floor. Maybe there had been a fight.

I opened all the doors, but there was no Jane. Then I came to a locked door. This could be it. This could be where Jane was!

I called out softly, 'Jane, are you there? It's me, Paul!' There was no reply. I stood back and kicked the door. As it crashed open, I ran inside.

I shone my torch around the room. Jane wasn't there - just a bed and an old chair. The cover on the bed was ripped and the chair was broken. I looked down at the floor. Suddenly I spotted something small and bright. I looked closer. It was Jane's ring, the one her grandmother had given her. No one else had a ring like that.

So I was right all along. Jane had been here. When I was outside calling to her, she was here in this dirty, messy caravan.

Jane would never stay in a place like this if she could get away. She was a prisoner. I was sure of it. Scarface and his friends had kidnapped her. They must have gagged her so she couldn't call out. Where was she now? Where had they taken her?

Anger and fear ran through my body. I picked up the ring and held it tight. A ring that fits well won't drop off on its own. Jane must have left it as a kind of message.

I could go to the police now. This ring was the proof I needed. There would be a big police hunt and Jane would soon be found.

I turned to go out of the caravan, but I was too late. A giant of a man was blocking my way. It was Bill and he had a knife in his hand. His wife was behind him. I was trapped.

Bill gave me an ugly look and held up the knife. 'Well, well,' he said, 'who have we got here?'

I shouted, 'Where's Jane? What have you done with her?'

Bill said, 'Jane? Who's Jane?' He turned to his wife. 'I don't know anyone called Jane, do you, my dear?'

She laughed. 'I don't know anyone by that name. Anyway, why should she be here, locked in our caravan? This man is out of his mind.'

A cold look came into Bill's eyes, and he held the knife close to my face. I could feel the point on my cheek. I said, 'What are you going to do?'

Bill laughed – a mean laugh. 'What am I going to do?' he said slowly. 'I'm going to send for the police!'

I could hardly believe my luck. That was just what I wanted. I could tell the police about Jane and show them her ring. This nightmare would soon be over.

7

A blue light flashed outside the caravan. The police had arrived. I was longing to talk to them.

Two policemen came up the steps of the caravan and I ran towards them. It was a silly thing to do. They thought I was trying to get away. They grabbed me and held my arms behind my back.

One of the policemen spoke to Bill. 'Don't worry, sir. We've got this young man under control. Now, what has he been doing?'

Bill said, 'He broke into our caravan when we were out. Then he went and kicked a bedroom door down. He smashed everything. Look at all the mess he's made. He must be mad.'

The policeman looked around. Then he turned to me. 'Did you do all this?'

'No!' I said. 'I did kick the door down. The rest of the mess was here when I came. I had to get in here. I was looking for my girl friend.'

'So your girl friend is in here as well, is she?' said the policeman. 'Did she make all the mess?'

I tried to make him understand. 'You must find her. Her name is Jane - Jane Bell. I don't know where she is. They kidnapped her.'

The policeman laughed. He said, 'Did you get that story from a book or the telly?'

'It's the truth! I've got proof that Jane was here.' I felt in my pocket. I was going to show him the ring, but I pulled out the ear-ring.

Bill's wife spoke up quickly. 'That's mine. It's just a cheap ear-ring. Fancy trying to steal a thing like that.'

Bill and his wife had made me look a fool. The police thought I was a crook. Every time I tried to tell them about Jane, they told me to shut up. They thought I was lying to get out of trouble.

One of the policemen went outside. I could hear him checking all the other caravans. Maybe he would find Jane. Then I thought, 'Would Bill call the police if Jane is hidden near here? No, he wouldn't. She's probably miles away by now.'

When the policeman came back, he gave me a push and said, 'Come on. We're all going down to the nick.'

He turned to Bill. 'You and your wife must come along as well, sir. We need a full statement from you so we can take him in.'

Bill and his wife looked worried. I knew why. They would have to give lots of facts about themselves, and they didn't want that.

Suddenly Bill's wife made out she felt sorry for me. It was a good act. 'He's just a young chap,' she said. 'He's upset because his girl friend has left him. We don't want to get him into more trouble, do we Bill?'

'That's right,' said Bill. He did his best to make his face kind and soft, but he looked about as kind as a man-eating tiger.

The policeman nodded. 'In that case, you may like to sort things out yourself. Maybe the young man could pay for the doors to be mended and for all this mess to be cleared up.'

Bill turned to me. 'How much money have you got on you?' he asked.

I took my wallet out. I'd taken all my money out of the bank before I came away. 'I've got £70,' I said. 'But that's all. I've nothing left in the bank. I need this money to look for Jane. I'm sure she's been kidnapped.'

The policeman glared at me. 'I'd stop that if I were you! These people are being very kind to you. Do you want to pay them, or shall I find a nice little cell for you down at the nick?'

I knew when I was beaten. I gave Bill £70. Then the policeman took my name and address and told me not to get into any more trouble.

I was broke, but at least I was not in jail.

8

I got back to my flat very late. I was too tired to eat. I just lay on the bed and went out like a light.

It was ten o'clock before I woke up. I had some breakfast. Then I went round to Jane's flat to see if there was any news.

The landlady was very kind. She knew I loved Jane and she wanted to help. She gave me a cup of tea, and I told her everything that had happened.

She said, 'I was shocked when Jane just picked up her things and left with that man. But are you sure she's been kidnapped? Maybe she's in trouble and she didn't tell you about it.'

I thought about that. Would Jane keep a secret from me? Maybe she would. After all, I didn't tell her about my fear of dark places.

'Have you been in touch with her mum and dad?' asked the landlady. 'They may know what's going on. I bet they'll help you.'

Jane's mum died a long time ago, but her dad was still alive. The landlady was right. I had to contact him. The trouble was, I had no idea where he lived.

'Have you got his address?' I asked.

The landlady smiled sadly. 'Sorry,' she said. 'All I know is he lives somewhere up north.'

Suddenly her eyes lit up. 'Just a minute', she said. 'I've got a postcard for Jane. It's from her father, Mr Bell. It came just after she left. It could be a clue for you.'

She went out of the room, and came back with it in her hand. It was a picture of a big hotel in Devon. On the back it said:

My dear Jane,

Having a great time here. The hotel is very good. It even has its own golf course. How is your boy friend, Paul? Please bring him up to see me when I get back. I'd like to meet him.

All my love,

Dad

So I had a clue. I could phone the hotel and talk to him. He might know what had happened to Jane. I prayed that he did.

It took only a few minutes to phone the hotel. I said, 'Please may I speak to Mr Bell? He's staying at your hotel.'

A man said, 'Hold on, please. I'll see if he's in.'

A short time later the same man said, 'I'm sorry. Mr Bell left yesterday. He was booked in for two weeks. But he had to leave suddenly.'

I said, 'I must speak to him. Did he go home? Please may I have his address?'

The man's voice suddenly became cold. 'I'm sorry, but I can't talk about my customers. I suppose you're trying to sell something. Well, I'm sick and tired of salesmen ringing this hotel!'

I said, 'You don't understand. I'm not a salesman.' But he put the phone down.

What could I do now? I should have known the hotel wouldn't give me Mr Bell's address over the phone. I had to go there myself. I had to talk to someone face to face.

But I had a big problem. The hotel was in Devon. Jane's father lived up north. I'd need lots of petrol. Somehow I had to get hold of some money.

I could ask the bank for a loan but that would take too long. I could sell something. There was my car. It was worth quite a bit. But without it, I'd be in even more trouble. Jane could be anywhere in the country. If I sold the car, how could I travel?

The only other thing I could sell was Jane's ring. I hated to part with it. I hoped Jane would see that I had no choice.

I found a jeweller's shop and rushed inside. The jeweller was very old and slow. How I wished he would hurry up! Slowly he looked at Jane's ruby ring. Then he said, 'Are you sure you want to part with this? It's worth a lot of money.'

I nodded and said, 'I don't want to sell it, but I must. Maybe I can buy it back later.'

I went out of the shop with a big roll of £20 notes in my pocket.

That ring made me think about Jane's family. She had told me they were well off, but I didn't really think about it. Now it sank in. Jane came from a rich family.

If only Jane had told me where her father lived. But she hadn't. I had to go to that hotel and get his address.

I thought to myself, 'I'll find you, Mr Bell. And then you can help me to find Jane.'

9

I got to the hotel about six o'clock that night. I went to the desk and told the man who I was. I said, 'Please will you let me have Mr Bell's address? I must speak to him. I think his daughter's life is in danger.'

The man said, 'Then you must go to the police. They are the only people who can help you. I'm sorry, I can't give you the address.'

He turned his back on me and went into a little office. I could see him working at a computer.

I tried once more. I put my head round the office door. I told the man a bit about Jane and said, 'Please help me.'

He wouldn't even look at me. He kept his eyes fixed on the hotel computer. 'Sorry, sir. I could lose my job if I gave you that address.'

Then I had an idea. Mr Bell's address would be on that computer. I was good with computers. It was my job. All I needed was two minutes alone in that office.

A plan was beginning to take shape in my mind. When the man came back to the desk, I booked a room for the night.

I went up to my hotel room and planned my next move. I knew what I was going to do, but I had to pick the right moment. Late in the evening would be best, about eleven o'clock.

The hours went by very slowly, but at last the time came.

I slipped out of my room. The hotel was very quiet. Just what I wanted. I went downstairs and crept towards the office. It was still open. Good. One man was sitting there. He was on duty, but he wasn't doing any work. He was just keeping an eye on things. There was no one else about.

I kept out of sight and went quickly into a room close to the office. It was the dining room. The tables were set ready for breakfast in the morning. No one was in there now.

I found what I was looking for: a fire alarm. It was on the wall close to the door. I took a deep breath and hit that fire alarm as hard as I could. There was a loud ringing all over the hotel. People started running and shouting.

The man ran out of the office. I heard him calling to the other staff. 'Hurry!' he yelled. 'We must get everyone out.' Then he dashed upstairs.

The office was empty. My plan had worked. I ran inside and sat down at the computer. In one minute I had the address. But I was still too slow.

The man came back and saw what I was doing. 'You again,' he said. 'You set that alarm off, didn't you? You must be mad.' Quickly he locked me in the room. 'That's got you,' he said. 'I'm calling the police!'

The only way out of the room was the window. It was locked. I picked up a chair and smashed it. Then I jumped outside and ran to my car. As I drove off, two fire engines came the other way. Just after them came a police car. Lights were flashing and a siren was going full blast.

I was in more trouble, but I'd got away. And I'd got Mr Bell's address!

10

I drove for most of the night. Then I stopped in a lay-by to rest. I slept for a few hours. When I drove on again, I felt cold and stiff.

I got to Mr Bell's home at about 10.15 a.m, I could tell Jane's father must be very rich. It was a big house with a garden the size of a field.

A man came to the door. It was Jane's father. I told him who I was. I told him about Scarface and Bill and his wife. I told him how I'd broken into the caravan. I told him about the ear-ring and the ring. I told him everything.

Mr Bell listened. He nodded his head as I spoke. I thought he believed me. Then he said, 'I'm sorry, Paul, but you've got it all wrong. Jane is quite safe. She just doesn't want to see you again. She's gone to stay with a friend. Please don't try to find her. Believe me, it's for the best.'

I said, 'But that just doesn't make sense! Jane loves me. She said she'd marry me! She wouldn't go off like that!'

Mr Bell said, 'Sorry, Paul, but that's how it is. Now please go. I'm waiting for an important phone call.'

I felt in my pocket and got out my wallet. I'd spent quite a bit of money, but there was still a lot left. I said, 'I sold Jane's ring to get here. I had no right to sell it. Please give her the money and say I'm sorry.'

I went sadly back to my car. So that was it. Jane had stopped loving me. She had left me for another man. I thought she was in danger. I thought she was a prisoner. But I was wrong. She just didn't want to see me again.

What a fool I was. The police were after me. I could end up in jail. And it was all for nothing. I thought about Jane. The way she used to look at me. The way she used to kiss me. Now my life had fallen apart. I sat in the car and tried not to cry.

As I sat there, Jane's father came out. He had a black case with him. His face was sad and tense. He got in his car and drove off fast.

Just then a man stepped out of the bushes by Mr Bell's house. He was tall and he had a deep scar on his cheek. It was Scarface. He didn't see me. He ran to a car and drove off after Mr Bell.

Why was Scarface here? Why was he following Mr Bell? Was he Mr Bell's friend? No. A friend doesn't hide in the bushes.

I sat in the car trying to sort it out. What was really happening? Had Jane left me, or was her father lying? How could I find out? Maybe Jane had sent a letter or a card to her father. If she had, it would be in the house. Right. I was going inside.

I found my way into Mr Bell's back garden. I was going to get into the house somehow. I had to know what was going on. I had to find out the truth.

I broke a window in the back door. Now I could open it. I went inside and looked all over for clues. I ran from room to room, but I found nothing. Then I heard a sound. It must be Mr Bell.

But it wasn't Jane's father. It was the police!

11

One of the policemen said, 'Now we know why you wanted
Mr Bell's address, don't we? You wanted to steal from him.'

I said, 'But you've got it all wrong. I wasn't going to steal
anything. I'm just trying to find out about my girl friend.'

The policeman smiled. 'I see. Well, you can tell them all
about it at the nick!'

At that moment the front door opened. It was Mr Bell.
He saw the policeman holding my arm. 'Please let him
go,' he said. 'I know him. He didn't come here to steal.'

The policeman said, 'But what about your window? And
what about the hotel window?'

Mr Bell smiled. 'The man's upset,' he said. 'He's lost his
girl friend. Please leave it to me. I'll sort it out with the
hotel.'

The policemen gave me an odd look and left.

'Thanks for your help, Mr Bell,' I said. 'But what is going
on? I'm right, aren't I? Jane is in trouble.'

He said, 'Yes, you're right. She's been kidnapped. They've got her locked up somewhere.'

He pointed to his case. 'I've just been to the bank. They want a lot of money. If I don't give it to them they'll kill Jane. If I tell the police, she's dead!'

All my worst fears were right. I said, 'Will they really kill Jane if you tell the police? Is it just a bluff?'

'No,' he said. There was fear in his eyes. 'They mean it. They've killed before. When they asked for the money, they sent me a box. I felt sick when I opened it. There was a woman's hand inside it.'

I stared at him in horror. He went on, 'Not Jane's hand, thank God. But it shows they'll kill her if I don't pay up!'

My legs felt weak. Scarface and his mates were killers. I grabbed hold of Mr Bell. 'Do you think they'll let Jane go? They may take the money and kill her anyway.'

'I know,' said Mr Bell. 'But what else can I do? It's the only hope. I must set off soon. They told me to go to Rushton Moor with the money. It will take me about twenty minutes to get there.'

Tears were running down Mr Bell's face, but he tried to smile. 'Let's hope for the best,' he said. 'If it's not a trick I'll be back in about an hour.'

'And Jane will be with you,' I said.

Mr Bell shook his head. 'No, Jane won't be with me. They've hidden her miles away from here.

Mr Bell picked up the black case full of money. 'I must go now,' he said. 'If I'm not back in two hours, call the police. Tell them everything you can. Give them Jane's ear-ring and her ring.'

'But I haven't got Jane's ring,' I said. 'Remember, I sold it.'

Mr Bell rubbed his hands over his eyes. He seemed to be cracking up under the strain. He was shaking like a leaf.

'Yes, yes,' he said. I forgot. Her grandmother gave that ring to her. It was a poison ring.'

A poison ring? What was Mr Bell talking about? Was he OK? He pulled himself together and went to the door.

'Goodbye, Paul,' he said. 'Give me two hours. Just two hours. Then call the police.'

12

I hoped Mr Bell would be back in an hour. But he wasn't.
The slow ticking of the hall clock was making me panic.
I had to find something to do. I got a bit of paper and
wrote down everything that had happened. That kept me
busy for forty minutes.

Time was running out. Scarface had tricked Mr Bell. I
was sure of it. Scarface must be laughing by now. He'd
got Jane. He'd got Mr Bell. And he'd got the money as
well.

Suddenly I thought of something. Mr Bell called Jane's
ring a poison ring. Did it mean something? I could fill
the time by looking it up in a book.

I ran to the library and found the kind of book I needed.
I turned the pages quickly. Poison ring. Poison ring.
Yes, I'd got it. I read the words out loud:

Poison rings *The first poison rings were made hundreds
of years ago. Their name comes from the fact that poison
was often hidden inside them. The stone of a poison ring
is like the lid of a tiny box. It will open up and . . .*

An idea had flashed into my mind. There might be something hidden in Jane's ring - a new clue or a message!

I didn't have time to think about it. Two hours had passed. Time was up. I had to ring the police now.

As I ran to the phone I tried to feel hopeful. But I just felt cold and empty. How could the police find Jane and Mr Bell? The hunt might go on for days or weeks. By then it would be too late.

I picked up the phone and tried to dial 999. Nothing happened. The phone was dead. Scarface must have cut the wires. So that's why he was hiding in the bushes.

I gave a cry of anger and flung the phone on the floor. No, no! I had to control myself. I said to myself, 'Cool down. Go out of the house. Contact the police. Go back to the jeweller. Get Jane's ring. See if she hid a clue inside it.'

It was just as well I'd written all the facts down. It would save time. I grabbed the pages I'd written and ran out to my car. I had to get to the jeweller's shop. I prayed that the ring had not been sold.

13

I drove at top speed. Then I slowed down a bit. If I got killed in a crash I would be no use to Jane or Mr Bell.

As soon as I saw a police station, I stopped and dashed inside. There was no time to hang about. I just ran up to the officer at the desk and gave her the pages I'd written.

'Read this,' I said. 'It's a matter of life and death.'

'Wait,' said the policewoman, 'you must...'

I was already half-way out of the door. I shouted, 'I can't stop. I'll phone you if I get any new clues.'

In two minutes I was in the fast lane on the motorway. My mind was fixed on Jane's ring. Was there anything inside it? Was I crazy to hope for a new clue? Had the jeweller still got the ring? Well, the miles were flashing by and I'd soon find out.

At last I got to the jeweller's shop. I rushed inside and asked to see the ring. Thank God it was still there. The ruby flashed red as the jeweller gave it to me.

With shaking hands I opened the poison ring. Yes, there was something inside it - a tiny bit of paper. And there was writing on it. It was what I had hoped and prayed for, a message from Jane.

I tried to read it, but it didn't make sense. It said: 'INGHSTTRN'.

Suddenly I knew what Jane had done. She had left letters out to make the message fit onto the tiny bit of paper. The real message was: 'IN GHOST TRAIN'.

So that's where Scarface and his mates had put her. Jane was inside the ghost train. Was she still there? Was she still alive? If I got there fast, I might be in time to save her.

I stopped just long enough to phone the police and tell them where to go. Then I was on my way to the fair. If I put my foot down, I'd be there in half an hour.

14

The fair was in full swing. The big wheel was turning. People were laughing and shouting. Kids were eating candyfloss and toffee-apples. Death and danger seemed very far away.

I looked round for the police. I'd hoped they would get to the fair before me. But there was no sign of them. Why were they so slow? Did they still think I was lying?

All around me there were happy faces. Killers were at work in the fair, but these people didn't know. I ran into the crowd and headed for the ghost train.

On the way I stopped a woman and said, 'Call the police. Tell them to go to the ghost train.' She smiled at me and walked on. I yelled to a man, 'Get the police. Tell them to go to the Ghost Train.' He nodded and went on eating his hot dog.

Soon the ghost train was in front of me. People were lining up to go on. Bill's wife was in the pay-box. It was just like any normal day at the fair.

Were the police on their way? Should I wait for them? No, it might be too late. I had to go for a ride on that train.

I remembered my birthday - the day Jane asked me to go on the ghost train with her. I couldn't face it then, but now I had to do it. I had to go into that dark tunnel.

Quickly I went to the pay-box. I kept my face turned away from Bill's wife and gave her the money. I felt sick and my legs were like jelly. A train came and I got onto it.

It was like going into a terrible nightmare. All my worst fears were coming true. The tunnel seemed to be closing in around me. I wanted to jump off and run out. Then I thought of Jane and how much I loved her.

15

The train went on and on into the darkness. There were the screams of ghosts all around me. Cobwebs brushed against my face.

I felt the train turn a corner. Suddenly it was light. In front of me a man was being killed in an electric chair. There was a big flash. The man's body shook all over. Then his head fell to one side. I looked on in horror. It all looked so real.

Then the train turned another corner. All was black again. Suddenly there was more light. This time it was a burning torch. Beside the track was an open coffin. All around were skulls and bones. Lying in the coffin was a young woman. A man was at her side, with a hammer and a wooden stake. As the train took me past, he drove the stake into her heart. Again, I stared in horror. Both people looked so real.

Then it was dark again. What would come next? The train twisted its way round yet another corner. There were more burning torches.

This time I was face to face with a row of heads. There were no bodies, just heads stuck up on poles. It was horrible. The heads were so life-like. They seemed to be staring at me. On the wall were knives and axes.

Suddenly I heard a woman screaming. It was Jane. I was sure of it. She was still alive. A man's voice called out, 'Don't kill her! For God's sake, don't kill her!' It was Jane's father.

Where were the voices coming from? There must be a hidden room. Quickly I stood up and jumped out of the train. I ran back along the dark, narrow tunnel to the row of heads. I tried not to look at them. I just grabbed one of the axes hanging there.

Jane's screams were very loud now. They were coming from behind the wall right next to me. I lifted the axe and smashed my way through. I was lucky. It was only made of thin wood and canvas. I soon got to the other side.

Ahead of me was a door. I kicked it open. Facing me was Bill. He had a gun in his hand. It was pointing straight at me. I froze.

Suddenly Bill smiled at me, as if I was an old friend. 'Why, it's Paul, the boy friend,' he said. 'You're just in time for the show. It will be good tonight. There are going to be some more killings!'

My eyes looked past him, into the room. It was just like an old torture chamber. Jane and her father were both there. Mr Bell was tied up. He was lying with his back to the wall. Jane was in a long dress. It was like one from a history book. She was tied down over a wooden block. A man with a mask stood over her, with a huge axe. It was Scarface.

Bill carried on talking. 'People call us mad, Paul. They think we are insane. They even locked us up for years. But we escaped. We're not mad, we're clever.

That's why so many people come on our ghost train. They love to be frightened. And we frighten them with real dead bodies. Did you see that man die in the electric chair? He was a real body. Good, wasn't it? So was the girl in the coffin.

Soon Jane will be on show to the public, just like the rest. Her head will look very pretty stuck up on a pole.

I've got a great idea for you and her dear old dad.
You're going to be shot by a firing squad, straight through
the heart.'

Shot through the heart. So that was how I was going to
die! There was nothing I could do to save myself. My axe
was no use against his gun.

Or was it? How good a shot was Bill? I turned the axe
sideways over my heart. Then I ran towards him. He
fired. The bullet hit the blade of my axe and shot up
over my head.

I didn't give him a second chance! I got to him and hit
him hard with the back of the axe. He dropped down on
the spot.

Then I turned to Scarface. He gave a loud roar and ran
towards me, swinging his axe.

It was Mr Bell who saved my life. He stuck his foot out
and tripped the madman up as he ran. His head hit the
floor as he fell and he passed out.

I heard shouts and people running. Suddenly part of the
wall crashed down. It was the police. They were here at
last.

A few minutes later we all came out into the sunshine.

There were lots of people standing around looking. An ambulance took Scarface away. Two policemen went with him. Then Bill was carried out. He looked a mess. There was blood all over his face.

The nightmare was over. My darling Jane was safe and so was her father. We looked at each other with tears in our eyes. They were tears of joy. I put my arms round Jane and we kissed. We were together now and nothing would ever part us again.